Books by Alberta Eiseman

From Many Lands
Mañana Is Now
The Sunday Whirligig

Gift from a Sheep

Gift from
a Sheep

The Story of How Wool Is Made

by
ALBERTA & NICOLE
EISEMAN

Atheneum   1979   New York

ILLUSTRATED BY TRACY SUGARMAN

LIBRARY OF CONGRESS CATALOGING IN PUBLICATION DATA

Eiseman, Alberta.   Gift from a sheep.

SUMMARY: Jenny raises a lamb; shears it; cards,
spins, washes, and dyes the wool
into yarn; knits a poncho; and wins prizes for her
spinning and knitting at the county fair.
Includes directions for making the poncho.
[1. Wool—Fiction]   I. Eiseman, Nicole, joint author.
II. Sugarman, Tracy   III. Title.
PZ7.E345Gi   [Fic]   79-10629
ISBN 0-689-30707-1

Text copyright © 1979 by Alberta and Nicole Eiseman
Illustrations copyright © 1979 by Tracy Sugarman
All rights reserved
Published simultaneously in Canada by
McClelland & Stewart, Ltd.
Manufactured by The American Book/Stratford Press
Saddlebrook, New Jersey
Designed by Mary M. Ahern
First Edition

To Margot

Gift from
a Sheep

JENNY JUMPED OFF the school bus and ran toward her neighbors' farm. She went there almost every afternoon, and today she knew they might be needing help. Several of their sheep were due to lamb; she could hardly wait to see the new additions to the flock.

No one was in the house, but in the barn Jenny found Tom and Jessica bending over one of the sheep.

"Jenny, I'm glad you're here. We were just talking about you," Tom said.

He stepped aside. Two tiny lambs stood before Jenny, newly born. One was already nursing, its little head tucked under its mother's belly. The other one just stood next to the ewe, looking forlorn.

"They were born just an hour ago," Jessica

said. "Two fine ewe lambs. The mother doesn't seem to want to nurse them both. We've been trying to hold the second lamb close to her, to see if she'll accept her . . ."

"At times it works," Tom added, "but it looks as if this little one will have to be bottle fed, and soon, too. She won't last long without some milk."

Jenny bent down to stroke the lamb. She had never seen anything as lovable, or as sad.

"Why won't she nurse them both?" she asked.

"It happens sometimes, if a young ewe has twins," Tom replied. "She recognizes the first born as hers, but not the second. Just feel the difference between them."

He took Jenny's hand and put her index finger gently in the first lamb's mouth.

"Feel how warm she is? Now try the second."

"Oh, the poor thing, she's all cold inside," Jenny said. "What can we do for her?"

"Well, for the moment, I'm going to give her some milk from one of the other ewes," Tom said.

"But it's hard, caring for a motherless lamb

when you have a whole flock to worry about,"
Jessica added.

She gave Jenny a long look. "We've been
wondering if you would like to bring her up as
your own. You've learned so much about sheep
these past few months, we both think you'd do
fine."

Jenny couldn't believe it. "My own lamb? How would I care for her? What would I feed her? What about the hours when I'm in school?"

Jessica smiled. "I wondered about that. Perhaps your mother would be willing to give the lamb a midday bottle, and you could do the rest."

"Does your family's goat give extra milk?" Tom asked. "That works very well for baby lambs."

Jenny thought that would not be a problem. Calamity, their goat, gave so much milk that Mother was always making cottage cheese and yogurt and trying to find new ways to use it up. But whether she would want another animal in the family now that she had a part-time job—what with the goat, the dog, the cat and kittens—that was something Jenny could not predict.

At first Mother said no, she really had too much to do to take on one more responsibility. Then Tom arrived, carrying the new lamb in his arms, and Mother melted.

"Oh, all right, I'll give her the noon bottle," she said to Jenny, "provided you're really sure you'll take care of the other feedings. It will be quite a task for you, you know," she warned. "Like having a new baby!" She sighed, but with a smile.

Jenny had never dreamed she would have her own lamb. She had enjoyed spending time with Tom and Jessica and their flock. She had refilled water buckets; brought fresh hay to the barn; held a bottle of medicine while Tom cared for a sick animal. Last year she had even helped some with the shearing. Best of all, she loved to watch Jessica at her spinning wheel. The way her hands turned the soft rolls of fleece into fine yarn seemed truly magic. And then she made such lovely things from the yarn: knitted scarves and sweaters and colorful woven fabrics.

Jenny loved the idea of making something to wear from wool sheared from her own sheep, so she named the lamb Lana, which means wool in Spanish. Still, it was hard to imagine that the soft, curly fuzz on Lana's body would ever grow into the thick fleece of a grown sheep.

The first time Jenny tried to feed her, Lana seemed frightened of the bottle held out to her.

"It's nice warm milk, Lana. You'll like it," Jenny said softly.

The little lamb backed off. Jenny dribbled

a few drops of milk on her mouth. The lamb
licked her lips, then stuck her tongue out again,
looking for more. Jenny pushed the bottle into
Lana's mouth and at the same time scratched
gently around her tail. Tom had told her to try
that: it was similar to the way a mother sheep
nuzzles her young while nursing. The trick
worked. Lana started to suck the bottle, weakly
at first, then gradually with more vigor.

After that, Jenny fed her pet several times a day and at night just before going to sleep. She made Lana a bed of deep clean straw in a corner of the barn; for the first few days the lamb stayed inside, but soon she was following Jenny wherever she went, even trying to come into the house and onto the school bus.

"She's just like the lamb in the rhyme you used to read to me when I was little," Jenny said to her mother.

At the end of a week, Jenny began to feed her lamb a little hay every day. Lana took to it gladly, bobbing her head up and down with each bite, as young lambs do. Then as the weather grew mild, Lana started to wander out into the meadow and nibble a little grass here and there.

Outside, she ran after anything that moved. She pounced at the cat and dog and at the goat, unafraid of her horns. Even when no other animal was with her in the meadow, she would sometimes leap into the air like a dancer; other times she would do a sideways slide. Jenny and her mother and father loved to watch the little lamb frolic and then, exhausted, collapse on the grass and take a nap.

Little by little, Jenny weaned her away

from milk to grass and grain. Each morning Jenny walked over to the little barn, filled a pail with fresh water, gave her sheep a fistful of grain and then let her out into the meadow. Whenever she was home during the day, Jenny went to visit Lana as she grazed, brought her an apple or some carrot tops from the kitchen, and scratched her fondly on the top of her head. She loved to stroke Lana's thick white fleece, growing longer and heavier as summer turned to fall.

Over the months, Lana grew and changed. By winter, she had developed into a large, gentle ewe, patient with the family dog, who licked her nose, with the kittens, who raced around her feet as she moved, even with the goat's two new kids, who liked nothing better than to jump on her back and bounce around on her soft springy fleece.

Jenny looked forward to spinning Lana's fleece. She was given a drop spindle for Christmas, and she was anxious to use it, but she knew that no shearing could be done until spring, when the weather was mild. Tom had told her that sheep can get sick if it turns cold or rainy right after they've been shorn. Meanwhile, she spent a good deal of time next door, learning as

much as possible from Tom and Jessica. Sometimes she brought Lana along to join the flock for a while. She worried at first about not recognizing her among the other sheep, but Lana always came running when she was called.

Finally spring seemed to settle in, one warm day following another. Tom came over on a sunny Saturday morning with his hand shears. They had agreed that he would do the most difficult parts, then Jenny would take over.

They brought down a large old bedspread from the attic and put it on the ground to keep the fleece clean. Then Tom lifted Lana's front legs and set her on her haunches: sheep cannot move in that position. Standing behind her, he supported her weight with his thighs. Lana let out a loud, unhappy ba-aa.

She looks just like an overstuffed armchair, Jenny thought, and she wanted to giggle, but she couldn't. She had watched other sheep being shorn, but for Lana it was the first time, and her eyes were wide and startled.

Tom started by carefully snipping the wool away from Lana's ears, down around her head and neck. Jenny held her breath. Without meaning to, she moved her hands in a cutting motion

along with Tom's. Mother stood by, a worried look on her face. Then Tom snipped down Lana's belly in a straight line, shearing the fleece away on one side of the belly, then the other.

He straightened up, took one look at the tense faces around him and burst out laughing.

"Don't look so worried! Lana isn't suffering! A bit cramped perhaps, but nothing more. All right, Jenny, it's your turn now. I'll hold her and you snip." He handed her the shears.

"Where shall I start?" Suddenly Jenny had forgotten everything she had learned, and she wasn't sure that she could keep her hands from shaking.

"Here, start with the shoulders." He guided Jenny's hand during the first few hesitant snips. Holding the shears in her own hand, Jenny could feel that it was only wool she was cutting, not the skin. She started to relax and handle the shears with more assurance.

"I'm all right now. I think I can do it by myself."

Tom moved his hand away and Jenny sheared along the right shoulder, down the leg, then in long cuts down the sheep's side to her backbone. She laid down the shears for a moment and rubbed her right hand with her left.

"Is your hand getting cramped?" Tom asked. "Would you like me to finish? We're almost there, you know."

"No, no, I can do it. Now the left shoulder, right?" She did the left side and the hind legs, then Tom took the last few snips and the fleece was free, one creamy, wooly mass lying on the bedspread.

"Let's check to see if we nicked Lana's skin," said Tom.

Jenny ran her hands along one side of Lana's body, then the other. The ewe felt strange to the touch without her wooly coat.

"Here's a small cut on her leg," said Jenny with concern. "And one on her neck, too."

"Don't worry, they'll heal quickly. Let's put some antiseptic on them," Tom suggested.

Mother brought a bottle of spray, and they sprayed the cuts so they would not get infected.

"Okay, now we can let her up," said Tom, helping Lana to get back on her feet.

The sheep looked around, shook herself, then took a few steps off the bedspread and looked around again. Within a few minutes she was nibbling some grass.

"Well, she certainly didn't seem to mind that too much," said Mother.

"You sound surprised. Sheep like to have their coat removed when it's warm," Jenny answered, "and they can't shed, like a dog or a cat."

Tom laughed. "Right you are! You did very well on your first shearing, Jenny. And look at the beautiful fleece you have."

Lana looked different without her fleece, small and much thinner. It didn't bother her, but the other animals were surprised by her appearance. Calamity the goat and her two kids came up all ready to butt the stranger, sniffed and decided the scent was familiar after all. The dog was just about to do the same when Jenny stopped him.

"Come on, Panda! It's just your old friend Lana in her spring coat. Don't give her a hard time!"

Panda sniffed too and decided there was no cause for alarm.

Jenny lifted up the fleece and shook it gently. It was heavy: about eight pounds, Tom said, and full of grease, a sign of a healthy sheep. She sat down next to the fleece and picked it clean, removing dried leaves, straw, sticks, bits of dried manure and a few burrs that had caught in the soft creamy wool. Now the fleece was ready to be carded, a process that combs and straightens the wool fibers before spinning.

Cards have curved wooden backs, wood handles, and wire teeth that all bend toward the handle. They look a lot like dog brushes, Jenny thought when Jessica lent her a pair and showed her how to use them.

Jenny started carding early the next morning, sitting outside in the sunshine. She pulled off a handful of fleece and placed it lengthwise on the top row of teeth, so the card was covered with a thin layer of wool. She took that card in her left hand and brushed the right card over it several times, with the handles pointing away from each other. With every stroke, bits of hay and dirt fell on her lap. How strange, she thought; before she started, the fleece had seemed quite clean.

When the wool looked straight and un-matted, Jenny pushed up with the right card over the left, so all the wool came off onto the left. Then with the right card she pushed the bottom end of the wool off the teeth of the left card and into the beginning of a roll. Then Jenny set the cards on the floor and with her hands stripped the wool off the card. The last step was to roll the soft, fluffy mass between her hands until it was the shape of a fat cigar, about ten inches long.

That was a rolag, ready to be spun, the first Jenny had made with her own fleece. She needed many more before she could start to spin, but finally she was on her way.

She laid the first rolag gently in a basket at her feet, then started on the next. Lana, who had been grazing in the meadow, came to her side and sniffed the fleece on the ground, then Jenny's fingers.

"Can you tell it's your fleece, Lana?" Jenny asked her. "It certainly smells like you! Or is it just that you want me to scratch you behind the ears?"

Maybe it was both, but Lana certainly seemed to want to stay close that day.

Jenny made twenty rolags that first morning, stacking them carefully in the basket so they would not crush. Her fingers felt the bite of the wire teeth now and again, and her blue jeans got scratched, but she was anxious to show her handiwork to Jessica, so she went next door with her basket and drop spindle.

"I know this won't make very much yarn," she told her friend, "but do you think it's enough for a start? I'd love to try spinning today."

"Sure it's enough. It will make a good spindleful of yarn," Jessica said. "I'll get you started and then you can take over."

Jessica took the drop spindle—a twelve-inch dowel with a round wooden disk at the bottom, like a child's top—and tied a piece of already-spun yarn to it. She carried this starter yarn below the disk, around the dowel and brought it up to the top of the dowel, where there was a notch; she caught the wool in the notch and formed a loop. Then she loosened the fibers of the starter yarn for an inch or two, mixed them with a few strands of fleece from one of Jenny's rolags and pinched them so they held together.

"Okay, now you're ready to go," Jessica said. "Hold the rolag in your left hand, with the spindle dropping below, pull out a few strands with your right, then twist the spindle clockwise, like a top."

Jenny twisted the spindle; it spun wildly, the fibers separated and the spindle fell to the ground. What a beginning!

"Gently! Don't twist so hard," Jessica said. "Wait, let me get my drop spindle and I'll show you."

"I didn't know you had one," Jenny said when Jessica returned. "I've always seen you use your spinning wheel."

"I used a spindle for a long time before I could afford to buy a wheel," Jessica said. "You can spin lovely yarn on the drop spindle, too; it just takes longer. In many countries that's all they use even today. You know," she added, "spinning wheels weren't even invented until the sixteenth century."

She took one of Jenny's rolags. Jenny winced. It had taken her so long to card those rolags, she hated to see anyone else use them. Even Jessica.

Jessica stood up, looped the rolag over her left hand, pulled

out some fibers and gave the spindle a gentle
twist with her right hand, then released it and
let it spin by itself. Then she slid her right hand
up to draw out some more fibers, all in
one smooth, continuous motion.

"All right, now let me try again," Jenny said. She pulled out some fibers from the rolag, gave a twist to the spindle, let it spin and quickly pulled out some more fibers.

"Relax," Jessica said. "Let the spindle work for you. Give it a firm spin, but gentle, and watch the twist rise up."

She was right. Jenny could actually see the twist run up the unspun fleece and twist it into yarn. Before she knew it, the spindle touched the ground. She had made yarn all the way from the hand that held the rolag to the floor!

"Now catch the spindle," Jessica said. "Slip the yarn from the notch and wind it around the dowel, then start again."

It sounded easier than it was, because the yarn started to untwist as soon as Jenny handled it, but then she caught it, wound it around the dowel and was ready to begin again.

"How much yarn do you think I made?" she asked.

"About three feet, I guess," Jessica answered, smiling.

"It's awfully bumpy, don't you think?" Jenny was disappointed in the way her yarn looked.

"Don't worry, you'll learn to spin it fine," Jessica reassured her. "Besides, bumpy yarn knits up into wonderful things. Have you thought about what you want to make?"

Jenny was silent as she struggled to attach a new rolag to the yarn. Then she set the drop spindle spinning again. The strands caught, held, and she could see yarn being made.

"One of my friends had a poncho that her grandmother knitted for her," she replied. "I'd love to have one like it. Do you think I'll have enough yarn from Lana's fleece for a poncho?"

"Oh, yes, more than enough. You can make a hat to match, too."

Jenny loved to knit, and the idea of making an outfit from Lana's fleece made her try to spin faster. Too fast, in fact: the fibers stretched too thin, the yarn broke and the spindle fell to the ground once more.

"Is that why it's called a drop spindle?" Jenny asked, picking it up.

"I don't think so, but I'm glad you can laugh about it," Jessica said. "It's a hard skill to learn."

She helped Jenny twist the broken strands together and start again.

It took several hours to spin just half the rolags she had made in the morning. Then it was time to go home, take care of Lana and help mother with supper.

During the days that followed, Jenny carded some more fleece and practiced spinning, but she knew that most of the work would have to wait until the end of June, when school was over. Then she would have long days in which to spin up all her lovely fleece and knit her poncho.

Meanwhile, she went with Jessica to collect materials with which to dye the yarn. They gathered black walnuts that had dropped from a big old tree last fall and brought them home. Then Jenny went to the supermarket and asked the produce clerk if she could have the onion skins at the bottom of the onion bin. He gave her a puzzled look, but when she explained that she wanted them for dyeing yarn, he let her take all she wanted.

As soon as school was over, Jenny set herself to spinning every day. At first she went over to her neighbor's, afraid that she would not be able to do it without help. After a week she felt more confident, as nice even yarn began to flow from her fingers. It felt like gold to her! She imagined herself dressed in Colonial clothes, carrying her drop spindle on the way to school. Did those children enjoy spinning as much as she did, she wondered?

The first time her drop spindle filled up and seemed too heavy, she unwound the yarn from the spindle onto the back of a chair, and made it into a skein.

She could have skeined all her yarn that way, but Jessica had an old-fashioned hand reel called a niddy-noddy, and Jenny wanted to try using it. It was a wooden implement shaped somewhat like an anchor, its three pieces set at curious angles. "Niddy-noddy, niddy-noddy/ Two heads and one body," went an old rhyme popular long ago.

Holding the niddy-noddy by the central rod, the "body," Jenny wound the yarn over and under, and made a dozen skeins of wool, each from one full drop spindle. Then she couldn't wait to see how they looked after they were washed.

She filled the bathtub with lukewarm water, added some of Mother's dishwashing liquid, carefully put the skeins in to soak and let

them stand for half an hour. When she came
back, she was amazed to see the amount of dirt
in the water. She rinsed the skeins, and the result
was magic. The yarn was unbelievably soft,
creamy white and so beautiful she wanted every-
one to come and see it.

She hung it up to dry in the shade, on a line
she had stretched between two trees, and stood
back proudly.

"Just look at all the lovely wool you gave

me," she said to Lana, who had wandered over to her side.

Mother was very impressed. "It looks so great just the way it is, I'm not at all sure you ought to dye it," she said to Jenny.

"I like it this way, too," Jenny replied, "but I do want to try dyeing some of it. Anyway, it'll be more fun to knit with some color."

A few days later, Jenny felt like a witch in a fairy tale as she stood by Jessica's stove with a long wooden spoon in her hand stirring a big pot of water, walnuts and skeins of yarn.

Most of the yarn was Jessica's; Jenny had put in only one of her skeins, and with some worry. She was afraid that it would harm the wool. They simmered the mixture twenty minutes, then took the skeins out and rinsed them in the sink, first in warm water, then cool. In that short time, the wool had turned a beautiful soft brown that harmonized well with the natural color of the other skeins, and Jenny was delighted she had tried.

Then it was time to use the onion skins, and with that, as with most natural dye materials, you have to use a mordant, a chemical substance that keeps color from fading. Jessica added alum to the water, then Jenny put in a bagful of onionskins and let them simmer for an hour. Then they added the yarn; when they took it out, it had acquired a deep golden shade.

"There are so many natural dyestuffs we could try," Jessica said. "Willow leaves, rhododendron, marigolds from your mother's garden . . . but I guess we've dyed enough for one day."

Jenny was all set to take her dyed yarn home so she could hang it up to dry when Tom walked into the kitchen to see how they were doing.

"That's beautiful yarn, Jenny, and the colors look great together. Have you thought about entering it in the county fair? I bet there aren't many people your age who spin so well."

Jenny hadn't even thought about the fair. She loved to go to it, but had never known anyone who exhibited. She told Mother about Tom's suggestion while she hung her dyed skeins on the line.

"I think it's a good idea," Mother said. "You should enter your yarn and perhaps you'll finish your poncho in time to exhibit that, too."

That spurred her on. Jenny took out the

directions she had found in a knitting book and set herself right to it. The directions called for knitting two rectangles of the same size and sewing them together so as to form a poncho. She took her measurements, then cut out a pattern from two large grocery bags slit open on one side. She tried it on to make sure it fit well, drew in several bands of color so she could include some of her dyed yarn, cast on the number of stitches needed to fit the pattern, and away she went.***

Some days, she took her yarn next door so she could knit while Jessica sat weaving at her loom. Other times she stayed in her own yard, knitting as she watched Lana graze. On a warm day, Lana would graze early in the morning, then look for shade and lie under a tree chewing her cud. Her fleece had grown back almost two inches, and she was starting to look like her former self.

"Maybe I should exhibit you too, Lana," Jenny said. "Wouldn't you like to win a ribbon at the fair?"

She sent away for entry blanks and filled

*** For complete directions, see page 43.

them out carefully, entering her own age and Lana's, and the articles she planned to show.

Jessica and Tom had never exhibited any of their sheep and were not sure that she should enter Lana.

"She is a handsome ewe," Tom agreed, "but I think there's a lot you have to know about showing animals at a fair. Still, as long as you're going to be there anyway, why not try?"

Jenny's knitting went quickly once she started working on it full time. Two weeks before the fair she had finished the poncho. Then she devoted herself to getting Lana ready to be shown. She trimmed her fleece in places where she had sheared unevenly. She practiced walking with her; that wasn't hard, since Lana was used to following her around. Two days before the fair she washed her thoroughly, using a bucket of water and liquid soap. After Lana had dried off in the sun, Jenny closed her up in the barn so she would not get dirty again.

On the big day, Jenny woke up before dawn. She ran to the barn to make sure Lana was all right. She swept the back of the station wagon and put down an old blanket, so the ewe would stay clean during the long ride to the fair. Then she took her poncho and the handspun yarn she was entering, wrapped them in tissue paper and put them carefully in a box.

By then her parents were awake, and Dad helped her load Lana into the car. After a hurried breakfast, they were off. Lana had never ridden in a car; she did not like it. Jenny did her best to soothe her, scratching her head and talking to her in a gentle tone of voice, but Lana baaad and tried to climb out of the rear window. Jenny closed it.

They passed a field of goldenrod in bloom, bright yellow in the early morning sun.

"How beautiful it looks," Mother remarked.

"Wouldn't that be a lovely color for yarn," Jenny said. "I wonder if it makes a fast dye. I must ask Jessica."

Father laughed. "Nothing will be safe from your dye pot any more!" he joked.

They kept on driving, Jenny growing more nervous with each passing mile. They reached the fairgrounds and asked for directions to the livestock barns, then found the youth division. A few pickup trucks were parked in front, each carrying several sheep. The boys and girls who owned the animals scurried around getting their pens ready, fetching buckets of water, carrying hay, presenting their credentials to the official in charge.

Dad and Jenny lifted Lana down from the station wagon. Lana looked slowly at all the activity around her and let out a long, pitiful baaa.

Jenny patted her on the head. "Don't worry, Lana, you'll be all right," she said, trying to sound more confident than she was.

She led Lana into one of the pens, holding her under the chin, as they had practiced. All around her, boys and girls were grooming their sheep for the judging. Some were trimming the fleece, others fluffed it up with special brushes that looked like cards. One boy cleaned his sheep's hoofs with a toothbrush; a red-haired girl put black shoe polish on her ram's hoofs.

"I had no idea you had to do all that," Jenny said to her mother.

"Well, it's your first time," mother reassured her. "You'll learn."

Jenny nodded, unconvinced. She gave Lana some hay and a bucket of water to keep her happy, then went off to the crafts pavilion to deliver her entries.

The fairgrounds were quiet and pleasant at that early hour; the public had not yet started to arrive. Jenny saw many boys and girls her age grooming their livestock; cows, pigs, horses and goats were being washed and brushed, curried and combed for their big moment in front of the judge.

The ladies in charge of crafts and needlework seemed pleased with what Jenny brought. They complimented her on her yarn and on the poncho.

"Where did you learn to spin so well?" one of them asked.

Jenny told them about Jessica and Tom and their flock, and about Jessica teaching her to spin.

"We're considering a spinning exhibition for next year," the lady said. "Perhaps you'd like to be part of it?"

Jenny was delighted to be asked and went back to the sheep barn where mother was keeping an eye on Lana. The pen next to Lana's was now occupied by two young lambs, small and curly and black all over, even their tongues. Lana kept her distance, unsure of what the two creatures might be. Jenny thought they were beautiful.

Then the officials called out the start of the judging. The sheep were classified by breed, sex and age, and their owners were divided by age, too: juniors up to fourteen years of age, and seniors, from fourteen to eighteen.

Jenny watched anxiously as each group was called. Boys and girls would go up to their pen, let out the sheep they had entered in that class and lead it before the judge. They would crouch by their sheep, eyes fixed on the judge, and hold the animal with one hand under the chin. Some of the sheep shifted around and bleated; others stood as if they knew exactly what to do.

The judge, a tall, thin man with a dark beard, walked slowly around every animal. As he approached, the boys and girls moved quickly to the other side of their sheep so as not to obstruct the judge's view. He ran his hands down each sheep's flanks, looked in its mouth and ears,

parted the fleece and looked inside it. Again he
walked down the line of animals and their
owners. Then he pointed to one sheep, a second,
a third. An official walked up and placed ribbons
on the three winners: blue, red, yellow.

"How come I never noticed these details
until today?" Jenny wondered.

Finally it was time for the grade classes, the groups of sheep that were not purebred. Jenny opened Lana's pen to lead her out. Lana balked and did not want to move. Jenny talked to her softly, and finally the ewe allowed herself to be led to the exhibit area. Jenny crouched next to her, imitating the young people around her. Lana objected with an indignant baaa. Another sheep replied, and then another, a concert of unhappy, restless animals.

The judge walked over and put his hands on Lana's back. She strained to get away from his strange touch. Jenny strengthened the hold under her chin, and wrapped her free arm around the ewe's rear end. The judge stepped back, to give Lana a chance to calm down, but when he came close again she leaped away, leaving Jenny sprawled out on the ground.

Several spectators tried to catch the runaway and missed. Jenny got up and ran after her, through a crowd that was gathering to see the commotion. Finally one of the older girls, who had shown her sheep in an earlier class, caught Lana by her hind legs and held her until Jenny arrived to lead her back.

The judge came over. "I guess she's never been exhibited before," he said to Jenny.

Jenny nodded and kept her eyes on the ground, fighting back tears.

"Don't be upset, she'll be less nervous next time," he said. "She's a beautiful ewe; try her again soon. You could do a bit better by her grooming," he added.

Jenny promised herself she would learn more about showing. She led Lana back to the pen, pushed her in roughly, made sure the gate was locked and went off to get her some fresh water.

"Not that you deserve it," she growled at her sheep as she set down the bucket next to her.

Then, with her parents, she walked through the crowd of fair goers to the pavilion where the crafts were exhibited. There, in the youth division, were her entries, and there were ribbons on them! Her handspun yarn had won a blue ribbon, her poncho a red, and prize money went along with both awards. The day had turned out well after all!

At closing time, they went back to fetch Lana and take her home. The ewe stood with her face close to the slats of the pen; she was bleating softly at the two little black lambs next door, and they were making gentle sounds at her.

"She's decided they really are sheep," Jenny said, laughing. "Wouldn't it be great to have a black lamb to keep her company? Then I could spin dark wool as well as white." She turned to mother. "I could knit you a tweed sweater, if you'd like."

Mother looked doubtful. "*Two* sheep?"

"Well, not right away, but maybe next year I could buy a black lamb," Jenny continued, "if I save my prize money and add to it."

She threw her arms around Lana's neck and planted a big kiss on her head. "We'll learn to do better at the next fair, Lana, don't you worry."

She placed her blue ribbon between the sheep's ears.

"It's really your prize, Lana. I owe it all to you."

Directions for knitting the poncho

Your PONCHO will be made up of two identical rectangles, which you will knit separately and then sew together.

The first step is to make a pattern that will fit you. To get the correct measurements, find the halfway mark between the end of your shoulder and the base of your neck. Ask a friend to measure the distance between that spot and your bent elbow, like this:

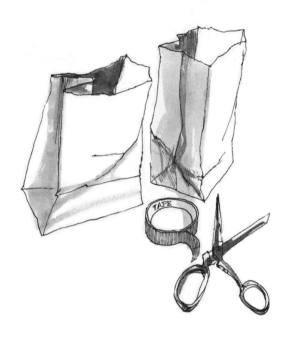

That's how wide each rectangle will be. To
figure out the length of the rectangles, double
the width and subtract two inches. Here's how
it works: if you're about 5 feet tall, your basic
measurement might be 14 inches. Your rectangle
will then be 14 inches wide and 26 inches long.
Don't worry about being too exact; ponchos are
meant to fit loosely, and you'll want to wear a
sweater under it when it's cold.

Now make your pattern. Take two supermarket grocery bags, the largest size. Slit them

open and measure off two rectangles the correct size, then cut them out. Mark them #1 and #2. Then tape the short side of #1 to one end of the long side of #2. This is how it will look:

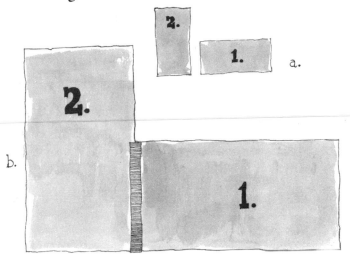

Now fold both pieces, so that you can attach the long side of #1 to the short side of #2. It sounds confusing, but when you do it it will seem quite easy. By then your pattern will resemble a poncho, like this:

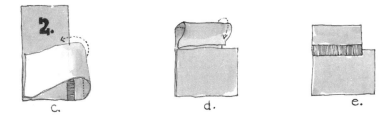

Slip the paper poncho over your head. Does it fit you? If it doesn't, you can cut out another one an inch or two larger, or smaller. The rules are the same. If you like the way it fits, decide if you want to add some color, and if so, where. Draw the stripes on your pattern with colored pencils or magic markers, so you'll get an idea of how it will look when it's finished. Now you're ready to knit.

First, you have to find out how many stitches you'll need to make an inch. That varies according to the thickness of your yarn and the size of your needles, and it's called finding your gauge.

To find your gauge, knit a small sample piece, maybe 2 inches wide by 2 inches long. Measure off an inch, and count how many stitches are in that inch. Now measure the width of your paper pattern and multiply the number of stitches in your gauge by the width of your pattern. (For example, if five stitches of your handspun yarn make up an inch, and your pattern measures fourteen inches, you'll be knitting a rectangle 70 stitches wide.)

Now cast on the correct number of stitches and start to knit. Every so often, hold up your knitting to your paper pattern to make sure of the fit. When you have finished one rectangle, cast on the same number of stitches for the second, and knit it to the same length.

Now you have your two rectangles, and you must join them together as you did the pieces of your paper pattern. First pin the rectangles together, or baste them loosely with a colored thread, so you can see how they look. Then sew them with the same yarn you have used for knitting, and pull out the pins or thread.

Your poncho is finished. Try it on and see how you like it. If you want a more finished look, you can add a row or two of crochet around the neck, and a fringe at the bottom. Then wear it, and see if anyone believes that you made it yourself!

Glossary

CARDING the process of combing and cleaning the fleece before spinning.

CARDS wire-toothed brushes with wooden backs used in pairs to comb and clean the fleece.

DROP SPINDLE a simple spinning device consisting of a wooden dowel inserted into a wooden disk.

DYE a substance used to apply color.

DYESTUFF any substance from which a dye is made.

EWE a female sheep.

FIBER each individual strand of wool fleece. The term is also applied to cotton, linen and synthetics.

FLEECE the coat of wool on a sheep, or shorn from the sheep.

FLOCK a group of sheep that stay together.

KID a young goat.

LANA Latin word for wool. Also used in Spanish and Italian.

LOOM a device used for weaving cloth.

MORDANT a substance used to prevent color from fading.

NIDDY-NODDY an old-fashioned hand reel used to wind and measure yarn.

PONCHO a short cape with a hole in the middle for the head, originating in Latin America.

ROLAG a roll of carded wool, ready for spinning.

SHEAR to cut the wool from a sheep.

SHEARS large scissors used on a sheep.

SKEIN a coil of yarn.

SPINNING to draw out and twist fibers together to form continuous yarn.

SPINNING WHEEL a device for spinning wool fibers into yarn, powered by a treadle.

YARN a long strand of wool fibers spun together.